Planting a Rainbow

Written and illustrated by
Lois Ehlert

Harcourt Brace & Company

SAN DIEGO   NEW YORK   LONDON

DEDICATED TO SHIRLEY AND DICK

Voyager Books is a registered trademark
of Harcourt Brace & Company.

Library of Congress Cataloging-in-Publication Data
Ehlert, Lois. Planting a rainbow.
"Voyager Books."
Summary: A mother and child plant a rainbow of
flowers in the family garden.
ISBN 0-15-262609-3
ISBN 0-15-262610-7 pb
ISBN 0-15-262611-5 oversize pb
[1. Gardening—Fiction.   2. Flowers—Fiction.
3. Mother and child—Fiction.]   I. Title
PZ7.E3225P1   1988   [E]—dc19   87-8528

Printed and bound by Tien Wah Press, Singapore

M L K

Printed in Singapore

Every year Mom and
I plant a rainbow.

In the fall we buy some bulbs

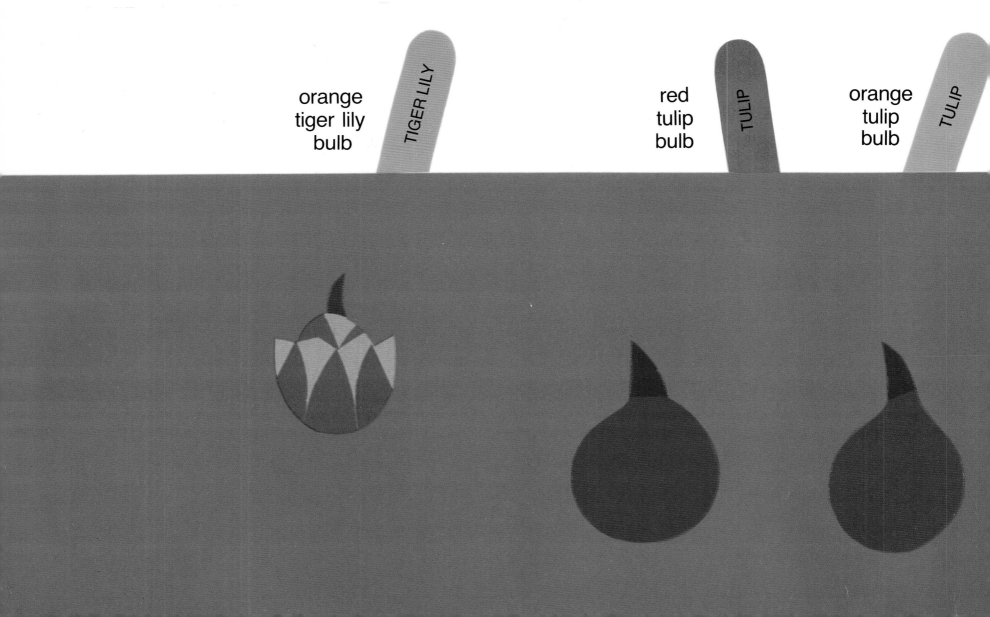

orange tiger lily bulb   TIGER LILY

red tulip bulb   TULIP

orange tulip bulb   TULIP

and plant them in the ground.

DAFFODIL

yellow
daffodil
bulb

blue
hyacinth
bulb

HYACINTH

purple
crocus
corm

CROCUS

purple
bearded iris
rhizome

IRIS

We order seeds from catalogs and

Phlox

Morning Glory

Zinnia

wait all winter long

Aster

Cornflower

Marigold

Daisy

for spring to warm the soil and sprout the bulbs.

TULIP

TULIP

DAFFODIL

HYACINTH

CROCUS

TULIP

TULIP

DAFFODIL

HYACINTH

CROCUS

Then it's time to go to the garden center to select some seedlings.

We sow the seeds and set out the

plants in soil,

MARIGOLD

ZINNIA

MORNING GLORY

CORNFLOWER

IRIS

PANSY

POPPY

FERN

and watch the

rainbow grow,

MARIGOLD

ZINNIA

MORNING GLORY

CORNFLOWER

IRIS

PANSY

POPPY

FERN

and grow,

and grow.

tulips

carnations

We have some red flowers

rose

zinnia

and
orange
flowers,

tulip

poppy

tiger lily

and
some
yellow
blooms.

daisy

marigold

daffodils

We grow something green

ferns

and
some blue
flowers,

morning
glories

delphinium

hyacinth

cornflowers

and some purple flowers, too.

crocus

phlox

iris

violets

asters

pansy

All summer long
we pick them
and bring them home.

And when summer is over, we know we can grow our rainbow again next year.